Dreams of the Pear Garden

AF590834

by Dale A. Johnson

Copyright © 2013 by Dale A. Johnson

All rights reserved.
This book, or no parts thereof, may be reproduced in any form without express written permission
Library of Congress Cataloging-in-Publication Data
Dale A. Johnson

Dreams of the Pear Garden

ISBN 978-1-300-49629-8

First Edition

Manufactured in the United States of America

New Sinai Press

Introduction

This small book came to me in a dream. It is a narrative of a haunting idea about bringing religious or spiritual ideas together. Most religious ideas are temporal interpretations of eternal truth.

The 8th-century Chinese emperor Xuanzong (also called Minghuang) established schools in the palace city of Chang'an (Xi'an) for music, dancing, and acting. There is a spirituality to all art. It takes us to a place of the wisdom of consciousness. These schools were a place for artists of all types: writers, poets, actors and musicians. In its entirety the school was called the Pear Garden (Liyuan). This tiny book is an expression of the spiritual and artistic truths of the Pear Garden.

The Author

Dreams of the Pear Garden

(excerpted from a book by the author Syncretism: Creativity and Consciousness in the Tang Dynasty, New Sinai Press, 2010)

A Short Story

Hello! I'm Gunner Wales. I have come to China in search of pears. A few years ago I bit into an Asian pear and its taste has made me crazy ever since. I know! I can get Asian pears at the supermarkets. It is not that kind of Asian pear I am talking about. You see I am talking about a poem about pears I read and savored until its taste was only a memory. I have been seeking to recover it ever since. Haven't you ever tasted something and it changed your life ever since. It might have been a celebration dinner or a piece of candy or the wafting fragrance of a food in the midst of transformation escaping from a kitchen. You do not even have to taste it. But you have to have it.

Ok, I know an Asian pear is really an apple. Frankly, when it comes down to it this search has nothing to do with Asia or pears. It is only a way to describe the search. Every search has to have an object. In this case it is a pear. The object is only a spot on the horizon like a Witness Tree. It is used for orientation.

So what is it I am searching for? What every human being who wants to be awake is searching for: truth, justice, and love you say? No, it is not even one or all of those things. It helps to go after that which you cannot taste, touch, or smell. No, it is emptiness. Yes, emptiness! So how does an Asian pear figure into this search?

It began at the Portland Art museum in Oregon. One afternoon I found myself waiting for a friend to go with me to Powell's Book store. They say it is the biggest used bookstore in the world. Maybe! I always found that a bookstore of any size is a good psychological test bed, especially on a date.

I met Beatrice on the internet so I asked her if she would go to the bookstore with me. My plan was that we would wander around and later have a cup of coffee downstairs in the coffee-shop. If she was interesting she would bring up ideas, authors, and books. The journey through the bookstore would either be paradise lost or regained.

Anyway, waiting for the experiment to start gave me a couple of hours to visit the art museum. They had a special exposition on Chinese art…you know….the Jade suit of armor, a Xi'an clay warrior and all that. I had this vague desire to find something. I just did not know what?

Once I paid the fee I heard the teller laugh under her breath. I did a double take. She looked down. I handed my ticket to a docent who was standing behind a velvet rope.

"Have a nice day!" she said.

"Why? I wondered. I have never had the courage to actually ask a person who says something so innocuous.

Immediately before me greeting my imagination was a print of a Tang Dynasty painting. Its background was an earth tone yellow. The only thing I knew about Chinese art was to read it from top down.

At the very top was a Chinese poem I could not read. Below it was a mountain seeming to float on yellow clouds. Set before it on a distant plain was the hint of color I recognized from childhood. It was a group of pear trees in blossom. In the foreground was a courtyard scene of men and women attending to various activities. Some were writing, others were studying scrolls, others were drinking wine, some were sleeping, and others were playing with dogs. It was a full cycle of life under the shade of pear tree blossoms. The brown fingered roots of exposed trees roots seemed to hold this scene in its wooden hands. The branch of a pine tree in the immediate foreground framed the painting.

I was deeply moved. It was a visual poem. I do not know why but I felt pulled into the painting as if I knew these people. I could taste the pear held in the hand of a grace filled women.

As a child I began to work on my father's farm at age six. We milked golden Guernsey cows. My mother grew a garden every year. After the evening milking in the summer when the light was warm and fading I walked through a small pasture to the house where dinner was waiting. I purposely walked through this pasture instead of migrating along the driveway in order to climb a fence and enter my mother's garden. In the corner was a pear tree. It had long since lost its white blossoms. Small, hard, green and rust spotted pears hung below small arrow shaped leaves. I loved eating these pears. They were not soft and juicy. One had to wait until the winter for them to turn golden brown and soft.

All these images and feelings came flooding back into my consciousness gazing upon this eastern print. It was then that I knew I would travel to China. How I knew this or why I thought it I cannot explain. It was prescient knowledge.

I turned left and shuffled my way to and through a series of rooms filled with crystal cased displays of weapons, clay pots, and glazed forms.

"Hello Gunner!" The voice was hushed but firm.

I looked up and to my delight I saw my friend Father John. John had been a spiritual advisor to me for many years. It was an informal relation but deep and profound. John was an extraordinary human being. He was a navy Chaplin for 30 years who retired and became a professional rodeo rider at an age when bones break far too easy. He was also an expert on Chinese Opera.

"I hear you are going to China" he said.

"Where did you get that information? I do not have any plans to go to China."

"I don't know. I heard it somewhere. Anyway, glad to see you. Do you enjoy the exhibit?"

I explained how moved I was by the huge print at the entrance of the exhibit. "I was actually thinking about you and some of our conversations when I was studying the print. Did you not tell me once those performers of Chinese Opera began in a pear garden?"

"Yes, in fact, even to this day members of the opera call themselves disciples of the Pear Garden. The Tang Emperor initiated the singing and acting troupe in a pear garden in a royal court yard in Xi'an, the Tang capital at the time." John's eyes danced in delight as he was getting louder and louder. People were beginning to state at us. Fortunately, John's wife came up and gave him a familiar tug on his sleeve. He shut up immediately. We walked together in silence to the next room.

"There it is!" he exclaimed.

"What?"

"The taste of the Pear." John was staring at a Tang Dynasty horse, neck arched, hooves prancing with delicate strength.

I held my breath.

Don't you see, if you don't believe it you can't have it!"

As if telepathically I understood what John was saying but it was probably the hundreds of hours we spent talking that helped me to understand, feel, and taste what he was saying. There is an inner aesthetic experience that is deeply spiritual. Gazing upon this horse one could see the love the artist had for his horse. Every hair seemed to be alive. The smell of sweat anticipating the liberation and freedom of travel could be sensed. Even the intelligence of this beautiful creature could be felt. It was as if this was a doorway to a world more real than our own. Beside us was a reconstruction of a royal Tang grave. Vessels, a chariot, weapons, and dried fruit were comforting the mummified corpse.

"No wonder civilizations buried their dead with items for the next world. They could taste it, feel it, and yearned to enter it."

"You got it son!"

We did not talk much after that exchange. Over the next hour we just kind of drifted apart. And then he was gone.

I thought about buying a book at the museum store but decided against it. In a few minutes I needed to leave and walk up to the Powell's books. I rushed over to Burnside street and crossed the street to the entrance of the bookstore where I had agreed to meet what I hoped would be my new friend. A few boxes of used books held down the sidewalk, obvious literary rejects that Powell's would not buy.

I looked up and there was Beatrice. Beatrice and I entered the glorious stacks of books. It was an entire city block and four stories tall. It turned out that Beatrice was a Zen Buddhist. She had just returned from a silent retreat where she sat for a whole week in disciplined silence.

"What did you learn from this experience?" I smugly asked. She smiled slightly. "It is not what you learn. It is about non-learning and quieting the mind. It is about entering the emptiness."

"You know I just had an experience where I felt connected to a consciousness where all experience felt richer and more real. At the same time there was a nonsensual feeling of emptiness. I do not know how to explain it in any other way."

We had a thrilling walk through the bookstore. I bought her a book on Zen Buddhism, a beautiful book about Guan Yin the goddess of Compassion. She did not want to accept it at first but I told her it was for the gift of spontaneous wisdom she gave me earlier. She did not want coffee and said she had to go. I thought I was getting a brush-off. But outside the store she reached into a brown lunch sack and extended her hand to me bearing a taste of heaven. "Pear?" she asked.

Discovering the Pear Garden

"Beatrice? What are you doing here?"

I was standing in line at the Hong Kong airport. I was ready to board the plane to fly to mainland China. I was being sent by a horticultural company to collect specimens of Asian pears to add to the genetic stock back in America.

"I just got a job teaching English in a university in China."

"Congratulations. Where at?" I asked.

"In Xi'an, western China." She smiled as if she knew something I did not. "Maybe we can sit together after the plane takes off?"

"Ok."

The plane was held up on the airstrip for about an hour. During this time I found myself seated next to an

American techie. I asked him how business was working out in China.

He told me about the problem his company was having with intellectual property rights. Technology transfers were occurring without payment. He was going to try to solve the problem. Apparently he was a lawyer too.

I asked him the Needham Question about why China had been overtaken by the West in science and technology, despite its earlier successes. Joseph Needham was a British scientist who worked for China during WWII. His works attribute significant weight to the impact of Confucianism on Chinese scientific discovery, and emphasizes what it describes as the 'diffusionist' approach of Chinese science as opposed to a perceived independent inventiveness in the western world. Needham's accusations against Confucianism can be seen as simply reflecting early Communist hostility to religion.

"It's a stupid question" he said. It is like asking why your name did not appear in today's newspaper. Besides you are looking at a blip in history during the time Needham was in China. I see the Chinese as very inventive and it did not stop even during the communist period."

"But I thought they just copy what the West as created?" I was puzzled.

"No, they take existing technology and improve or transform, or readapt it" he said.

"Sounds like copying to me." I was pleased with my response.

"Thomas Edison, America's greatest inventor did the same thing. He took existing technology and improved or readapted it. Name one inventor who did not do the same. Edison stole ideas from his employee Tesla who actually was a greater and more original inventor. We all stand on the shoulders of those who have gone before us."

"You mean pick the pocket of others the way you are describing it" I countered.

“Perhaps, but genius is more often taking something old and giving it new use. The Egyptian Pyramids have children’s toys with wheels a thousand years before someone applied it to full sized ox carts.”

This was turning into a smack-down. This attorney/techie had clearly thought about this subject much more than me. I was relieved when the plane took off and Beatrice came and sat in an empty seat on the other side of me. I turned my attention to her and began blabbing about the virtues of plant genetics. She could have cared less but at least I could maintain a superior sense of self instead of being crushed by the arguments of the lawyer next to me.

Finally Beatrice began to breathe slowly, her eyes half closed, and nearly whispered, “Ever heard of morphogenesis?”

“What?”

“Morphogenesis… the way in which plants assume form. Apparently the genes of plants, crystals, or humans cannot be predicted by the information of genes. I thought you were a horticulturist?" Now she seemed to frown.

"I am but I thought morphogenesis is biologically determined." I was sure she was going to spring something on me.

"Rupert Sheldrake is my distant cousin. He says there is a morphogenic field that is a kind of field of consciousness…a collective consciousness if your will." She was getting excited. I thought I would put a stop to this nonsense."

"No one accepts his theory" I said with certainty.

"I do…..there is a kind of morphic memory that feeds the present. Haven't you ever noticed that in the greenhouse that it might very difficult to get certain cuttings started if they have never been grown before? But once you grown them it is much easier thereafter?"

"As a mater of fact I have noticed this phenomenon. There is a kind of syncretizing the way a computer syncs with other devices. Once it locks in then there is a free flow of information. I do not know why this happens but there seems to be a kind of conservation of form…a field of information that draws the seed toward a certain form in the future. I just figured all this information is contained in the gene."

"Nope. There is a kind of syncretic action that arises out of a field of information but it is not material." Now she was beginning to bully me.

"Well you are not a real scientist then" I huffed.

"Never said I was."

I couldn't get off the plane fast enough. I am a scientist and this was way too much for me.

Xian airport was small but efficient. A colleague picked me up and we drove to into the city. His name was Walt Benson. He was a farmer's son who went to Washington State University and got a Ph.D. in agronomy. He was a specialist in Asian Pears and had searched the world for a super variety. He believed he found one and my job was to bring specimens back to the West Coast of the United States and test this super variety for adaptability in the States.

On the way into the city Walt asked, “How would you like to go to the Opera tonight? Got some tickets.”

“Didn’t know they had opera in China.”

“This is Chinese Opera. It is quite interesting. Might be a nice introduction to China.” Walt smiled.

“Sure. Sounds good to me.”

Once we checked into our hotel, Walt called me on the phone. He gave me directions to the hotel dining room downstairs. When I got downstairs I could not believe my eyes. Sitting next to him at the table was Beatrice. Great, another wasted hour of useless talk. I was hoping to get to work with Walt.

"Hey, this lady says she knows you" Walt shouted across the room.

I nodded not wanting to have people stare at us anymore than they were staring.

"Hello Beatrice." I could hardly look at her.

"Ok, I know you think this is a setup but it is not. Walt and I met a few minutes ago just by accident. You know, six degrees of difference. Just a coincidence."

I was speechless and annoyed. I was even more annoyed when Walt told me he invited Beatrice along to the performance of the Peking Opera.

Turns out that Walt was a big fan of the Story of the Monkey King. This was the story the Peking Opera was performing that night.

The theater was not spectacular I ended up sitting next to Beatrice and I was glad I did. The Story of the Monkey King was about a supernatural Monkey who travels with a Buddhist monk to India to recover ancient scriptures.

Guan Yin rescues the Monkey King and eventually this impish creature is transformed into a human being. What struck me though was not so much the story but the staging. Blossoming Pear trees adorned the stage. In fact in the printed program it said that professional performers of the Opera call themselves, 'Disciples of the Pear Garden.' Apparently Chinese Opera began during the Tang Dynasty in the royal courtyard's Pear Garden. I had to laugh and I leaned over and whispered, "I see why you brought me here." Walt seemed a little puzzled.

After the Opera we went to a Tea House. We were ritually served tea. In a way it was like the Opera where every gesture, movement, color, odor, and instrument had a meaning and was part of a sacred order. I still didn't know what it all meant but Beatrice was a big help. I asked her about the story of the Monkey King and what the story meant.

"Did you notice that it was all interplay of competing and cooperating forces, Strategies of redirection, adaptation, mimicry, camouflage, false signals, and predatory warfare were all going on throughout the adventure." She waited for an answer.

"Kind of like our lives" I laughed.

"Yah, and they are all being practiced here in China." said Walt, I just got an email from the nursery that they have jumped the price on us and are delaying our visit.

"What do you suggest we do?"

Beatrice chimed in and said, "Wait it out. In the meantime I know of an ancient orchard out of town about 30 miles. They are not very professional but we could go visit them tomorrow while we wait."

Sounded like a wild goose chase to me but it was a way to kill time.

The next day Walt and Beatrice met me in the lobby. Beatrice had arranged a van for us. We drove for about an hour until we were deep in the mountains. The driver made us get out and told us to get on motorcycles. The road had changed into a dirt path. Frankly I thought we were going to get robbed. We rattled our way up an even higher mountain past tiny orchards and gardens. We then walked another couple miles until we arrived at the most beautiful orchard I had ever seen. We were in a mountaintop valley; fog was spilling over the western rim. A late morning sun was rising through it.

A tiny Chinese farmer emerged among the trees with a walking stick in one hand. He spoke perfect English. Turned out that he had graduated in philosophy from Cambridge. He and Walt talked for a short time and then Walt turned to me and said, "He wants to take us to the Pear Garden."

"Great, let's go" I said although I frankly wondered how much a philosopher could know about plant genetics of Asian Pears.

"There is a catch though" said Walt, "We have to pray first in the family shrine."

My heart was beginning to sink but I was resigned to show a bit of grace before the reward. It was my dream to find this pear garden.

We followed the old man to the side of a hill. He unlocked a gate and we entered a cave which was more of a crevice in the cliff underneath an overhang. The limestone formation was a huge massif of soft stone. As my eyes adjusted I could see hundreds of figures. In the very center was Guan Yin with a thousand arms. Beatrice began to explain the names and purposes of all the forms. It was clear that it was a mix of figures. Taoist, Confucian, Buddhist, Christian, even an image of Mani who created a Buddhist/Christian religion in Asia where it was popular in Afghanistan, Persia, and western China.

After what seemed like endless hours of praying, banging drums, bells, and lighting incense I smiled asked the old man, "So where is the Pear Garden?"

"It is here!" He turned and surveyed the images. I cast a furious glance toward Walt. But then I thought that maybe he misunderstood.

"No, the orchard where the Asian pears are located. Is it nearby?"

"It is as close as your heart."

Well I had about enough of this non-sense. I felt I had been tricked into praying and I just wanted to go back to the hotel.

Then Beatrice pointed to the altar of Guan Yin. "Didn't you notice?"

There upon the altar was an Asian pear of exquisite shape, color, and size.

The old man walked over to the altar, bowed and picked up the pear. He took out a knife and sliced off a piece of pear. The way he did it reminded me of my father who was also a farmer. For some reason this triggered a sense of calm in me. He handed the pear to me and said, "A gift from Guan Yin."

The pear slice contained a seed. It sat on top of his fingers like a crescent moon. "Please, eat the seed too. It is good for your health. The bitterness will be transformed once inside."

Now I knew there was a Pear Garden. I politely ate the pear slice. I could tell this not only was a true act of hospitality but it also was an act of love. I sensed this was a man without guile. He was allowing me to enter a special world.

We did see a pear garden that day but it was a kind of anti-climax. This was an extraordinary man we had met. One\ the way out to the road I asked him a bit more about his education. He did know a lot about horticulture, perhaps as much as me. I probed a little further. "What did you do your dissertation on at Cambridge?" I was curious to know how a philosopher could know so much about pears and create such a beautiful pear garden.

"I wrote an answer to the Needham's question as to how will China come roaring into the 21st century as an innovative, compassionate, and scientific world leader? My answer is by re-invoking a previous cultural and religious principle of the Tang Dynasty: "

"Which is?" I asked.

"What I practice every day in the pear garden of my heart and field: "SYNCRETISM!"

That night I had a dream that the pear seed sprouted in my heart and grew into a tree adorned with fruit of many kinds.

The End

ThreeFriends

Bamboo
Good morning my friends
night winds have not broken you
leaves touch frozen dew
Plum
Blossoms praise the sun
The new hidden in the old
Secret life unfolds
Pine
Eternal color sings
the patience of the ages
as the wind rages

早上好，我的朋友
寒风没有破坏你
叶触冻露

开花赞美太阳
新的隐藏在旧的里
展开秘密生活

永恒的颜色歌唱
耐心的年龄
风肆虐

A Scholar's Friends

Bamboo

My friend, the bamboo, you bend to the wind but do
not break.
Your center is hollow yet you are full of humility
Why do you not wither in the winter
when so many others die?

Plumb

Your friend the plum holds a secret too
She holds within her a girl's beauty
Yet she appears brittle with age.
Like one who conceives when old

Pine

Perhaps our friend the Pine can answer us
Is it your friendship that keeps you alive
The immortal plum and the patient pine
when snows hang heavy on your branches?

我的朋友，竹，你向风弯腰，但不会被摧残。
你的中心是空的，但你是充满谦卑
你为什么不在冬天枯萎
当这么多的人死亡？

你的朋友梅也持有秘密
她隐藏在女孩的美丽中
然而，随着年龄的增长，她显现脆的。
就像一个孕育新生的老人

也许我们的朋友，松树可以回答我们
是你们的友谊，让你活着吗？
不朽的梅花和耐心的松
当沉重的积雪压在**分枝上**吗？

Other books by Dale A. Johnson

Available at Amazon.com, Barnes and Noble, and Lulu.com/barhanna, distributor of the New Sinai imprint.

Science Books

1.Anachrology
2. An Incomplete Guide to Small Blue Butterflies of Southwestern China
3. An Incomplete Guide to the Butterflies of the Dominican Republic
4. Field Notes on Martian Life
5. Einstein at Prayer, Jesus in the Lab

Detective Series

6. Columbia River Murders
7. Mahjong Murders
8. Laowai Murders
9. Guan Yin Murders
10. Mahjong Murder Mystery Series

Fiction

11. Festschrift of Fiction
12. Little Stories from the Monastery Between the Mountain and the Sea
13. Twin of Jesus
14. Stories of the Temple between the Mountain and the Sea
15. Syncretism: Creativity and Consciousness in the Tang Dynasty
16. Women without Faces

Humanitarian Studies

17. Release the Hero Within
18. Why Should We Care?
19. Altruism: Serving Others

Cookbook

20. The Great Fast Cookbook

Monastic Studies

21. A Rule for Community

History

22. Following the Sun
23. Visits of Gertrude Bell to Tur Abdin
24. Chronicle of Joshua of Zuqnin
25. Asian Jesus in China
26. Asian Jesus
27. Asian Christ
28. Asian Christian
29. The Asian Faces of Jesus
30. Following the Sun
31. Monk George and his Debate with Muslims
32. Jingjiao: Luminist Religion of China
33. Luminous Stones: Christian Inscriptions in Ancient China

Inspirational

34. Wake Up! Pay Attention
35. Release the Hero Within
36. Your Life is None of Your Business
    Published in Chinese:Life is None of Your Business (China Edition)
37. Lives of Gratefulness
38. Forty Meditations by Father Dale
39. Bamboo Dreams
40. Hospitality

Barhanna Monograph Series

41. Barhanna Monograph Series
    42. The Syriac Codex Computers
    43. The Goodspeed Syriac Fragments
    44. Syriac Fragments of MS. Balamand 15
    45. The Jesus Caves of China

46. Arab Christian Art of Balamond
47. Barhanna Monographs, Vol. 2

Biography

48. Fire on the Mountain
49. Is God Dead Yet? I hope so!

Syriac Studies

50. Syriac Genius
51. Syriac Influences in Western History
52. Living as a Syriac Palimpsest
    Republished as: Dominican Palimpsest
53. Syriac Studies
54. Asian Christ
55. A Gospel Harmony
56. Daily Prayers from the Language of Jesus
57. Tracts on the Mountain of the Servants (hagiography)
58. Divine Liturgy of the West Syriac Traditions
59. Ancient Aramaic Hymns of Christianity
60. Monks of Mount Izla
61. Corpus Gradum
62. Hilaria: A Woman Who Became a Man

Intra-religion Studies

63. Christ Mind, Buddha Heart
64. Jesus on the Silk Road: Essays on Christianity in China, Mongolia, and Asia Minor
65. Soft Like Water
66. A Disciple of the Pear Garden
67. Wisdom is Not What You Think
68. Searching for Jesus on the Silk Road

A Life without Limits Series Book

frbarhanna@yahoo.com

Credits

Bamboo, Pine, Plum
Artist: Han Shiao, p. 30

Bamboo
Artist: Shi Kao, p.32

Birds and Snow Plum
Artist: Chyan Kang Sh, p.33

www.ingramcontent.com/pod-product-compliance
Ingram Content Group UK Ltd.
Pitfield, Milton Keynes, MK11 3LW, UK
UKHW020215250726
13967UKWH00001B/8